THE ELF OF THE ORCHARD

"Merrily, merrily, shall I live now,
Under the blossom that hangs on the bough."

ARIEL, *in "The Tempest."*
(Shakespeare.)

The Secret. p. 38.

THE ELF OF THE ORCHARD

BY

ALICE P. MOSS (MRS. NOWELL PRICE)

AUTHOR OF "THE DREAM GARDEN"

ILLUSTRATED

BY

SYBIL BARHAM

AND

ELIZABETH PEACOCK

LONDON

WELLS GARDNER, DARTON & CO., LTD.

3 & 4, PATERNOSTER BUILDINGS, E.C.

PRINTED IN GREAT BRITAIN
WELLS GARDNER, DARTON AND CO., LTD.

HUGH NOWELL,

HIS LITTLE BROTHER,

AND ALL LITTLE CHILDREN WHO LOVE

FLOWERS AND FAIRIES

CONTENTS

LIST OF ILLUSTRATIONS

COLOURED PLATES

THE ELF OF THE ORCHARD

CHAPTER I

THE ELF'S STORY

THERE is certainly no time of the year like the time when the fruit-trees are in bloom, and there is no place in all the world half so beautiful as the old orchard at the end of the garden.

At least, so thought Miss Wide-awake as

she trailed through the long grass one sunny morning and seated herself and her whole family of dolls under the big apple-tree.

The grass in the orchard was very green, and it made a lovely soft carpet for Miss Wide-awake; while overhead the branches of the apple-tree formed a roof of pink and white, more like a fairy palace than anything else.

Through the snowy boughs one could see little patches of blue sky, which looked like oddly-shaped windows, and every now and then the wind would move the branches ever so little, causing a whole shower of petals to fall like snowflakes over everything.

Miss Wide-awake tried to catch the blossom as it fell rustling to the ground; some of the petals were pure white, and others had a tint of rose colour; these dropped from the old gnarled apple-tree under which she sat.

"All the trees look as if they were dressed for a wedding," she said. "I wonder whose wedding it can be?"

Miss Wide-awake often talked to herself and asked questions like this, but as a rule she got no answer. To-day, strange to say, quite a number of voices answered her.

She could not tell where the voices came from, for they all seemed to be speaking at once, and Miss Wide-awake began to feel very confused, when just at that moment another shower of blossom fell on her, and a tiny little voice at her elbow said:

"Listen to me. I can tell you all you

want to know !" And turning her head, she saw a quaint little creature seated on the grass at her side.

It could not have been more than two inches high, with a face like a crumpled bit of apple-blossom and a body no bigger than the stem of a leaf.

"I am the Elf of the Orchard," said the tiny stranger. "In fact, this orchard really belongs to me."

Miss Wide-awake was greatly astonished to hear this, because she had always thought that the orchard belonged to her father.

"Now, as I know the place very well, and all the ins and outs of it, I can tell you many things that you have very likely never heard of before."

Miss Wide-awake was just about to thank the Elf when he stopped her :

"Don't speak!" he said; "all you have to do is to listen. I should think you are just about young enough. The younger you are, the better you are at listening to the things I have to tell you. Grown-up people can't listen at all; they are either too deaf, too stupid, or too busy—generally too busy. Babies are the best of all. They can listen for hours together. Haven't you seen them cooing and smiling to themselves? That is when the fairy people are telling them stories, and when they cry, and you can't find out the reason, it is nearly always because the goblins are telling them bad stories, and they don't like it. But it's not only the fairies and goblins—nearly everything has a story to tell. In this orchard, for instance, there are stories being told all day long. Can't you hear how full of voices it is? First there are the Birds, they have the most wonderful tales to tell, and the Bees repeat the same one over and over again ; while the Brook down there has been telling its story for over a thousand years, and hasn't come to the end of it yet. Then there are the Rushes, they are always whispering to each other, and the Wind brings a fresh yarn every day. Why, if all the stories that are being told in this orchard were written down, they would fill a million books in no time ! I've got a story of my own, too ; would you like to hear it ?"

"Very much," replied Miss Wide-awake, who was beginning to feel quite at home with the Elf. "But, first of all, I should like to know how you got into this orchard at all ?"

"That's what my story is about," said the

Elf. "I came here on business—very important business. You see, it was somebody's birthday."

"How did you know it was?" asked Miss Wide-awake.

"I didn't know until I got here. It happened like this. The Fairies asked me to take a present to somebody, and whenever the Fairies send a present to earth, it means that somebody has a birthday."

"But what was the present?"

"Ah!" said the Elf, "that's the strange part of it. You'd never guess. There's a corner in the Fairy Garden where they grow, all pink and white and ever so pretty. Now, I happened to be passing one day when I heard the Fairies saying it was time for somebody to have a birthday, and someone must take the present."

"I thought presents always came by parcel post," said Miss Wide-awake.

"Not this sort. The Fairies bring them themselves; but as everyone seemed so busy on that day, they asked me to go.

"'But I shan't know who to give it to,' I said.

"'Oh yes, you will,' answered the Fairies; 'there are so many people on the earth wanting birthday presents, you will easily find someone to leave it with.'

"Well, I took the present and flew down to earth, and began to look about for someone to give it to. I saw a great many people who were very busy, and many others who looked very sad. They *all* seemed to be wanting something, and the hard thing was to choose somebody who wanted the Fairies' present most of all.

"I wandered about for a very long time, and at last I came to this orchard.

"A lady was walking up and down under the trees, and of all the people I had seen I thought she looked as if she needed a present most. Her face was so gentle and kind, I felt sure she must be the right person to have a present, even if it wasn't her birthday; so just as she was passing beneath me, I dropped it right into her arms. She did not look at all surprised, only very, very happy. Any-one else would have said it was just a bit of pink and white blossom that had fluttered down from a branch overhead, but she and I knew better than that."

"Then what was it?" asked Miss Wide-awake.

"A flower from the Fairy Garden, where they grow the things that people want most."

"But whose birthday was it?"

"Why, yours, of course; the very first one you ever had. That's why you don't remember it."

"Under the big apple-tree," p. 2.

CHAPTER II

THE MOONFLOWERS

"THEY must grow *somewhere!*" said Miss Wide-awake.

"Of course they do," answered the Elf.

"Then why have I never seen them?"

"Why? Ah, the reason is simple enough! You come out into the garden when the sun shines and you see—sunflowers. Now, if you came out in the moonlight you would be quite sure to see—moonflowers."

"Do you really think I should?"

"There's not a doubt about it. I *know*, because I've seen them myself."

"Oh, how I should like to see them! But I never shall, because I'm not allowed out after dark."

The Elf looked very wise and kind.

"No, of course not," he said; "but it's a pity, because you miss a great deal that way, a very great deal. But I think I can manage it somehow about the moonflowers. I might come and fetch you some night when they are out in full bloom. No one would miss you if you were out with me."

Such a friendly offer as this was not to be despised, and Miss Wide-awake willingly agreed to go with the Elf any night he liked to come for her.

"Let's fix it, then, for Wednesday week," he said, for he was a very prompt person, although he was an Elf. "It will be full-moon then, and the moonflowers are certain to be out, only *don't tell anybody.*"

Miss Wide-awake promised this readily enough, for indeed there was no one to tell, except grown-up people ; and, as the Elf said, they were no good at listening to anything about elves and moonflowers.

When Wednesday came, Miss Wide-awake went to bed as usual and to sleep, but her dreams were not at all the usual sort of dreams.

She had not been asleep very long before she heard a well-known voice saying:

"Miss Wide-awake ! Miss Wide-awake !

Have you forgotten all about the moon-flowers ?"

Of course she hadn't forgotten, and in less time than it takes to tell you, she was out of bed, and right out in the garden. It was a very warm, still night, and a big round moon was sailing overhead, making everything look bright and shining.

Miss Wide-awake thought that the garden was far prettier at night than in the daytime, for the lawn was like a large piece of the silver paper that comes out of chocolate-boxes, and the garden paths looked like broad white ribbons. Even the Elf himself seemed bigger and more important than usual as he skipped along at her side.

" But where are the moonflowers ?" asked Miss Wide-awake.

" Round the corner ! Round the corner !"

replied the Elf cheerfully ; and on they went, threading the mazes of the garden-paths until they came to a flower-bed by the hedge which separated the garden from the orchard.

There, sure enough, by the pale moonlight she saw a row of tall and stately flowers quite unlike anything she had ever seen before.

They were all of a bright silvery shade, and every petal was shaped like a new moon.

"There !" cried the Elf; "aren't they worth coming to see ?"

"Oh !" gasped Miss Wide-awake, "they *are* beautiful ! May I—oh, do you think I may pick one of them ?"

"No," replied the Elf sternly, "I don't think you may."

"But I want one so much—only one !" pleaded Miss Wide-awake.

"That's so like a human being," grumbled

the Elf; "they can't admire anything without wanting it."

"Well, what's the good of flowers at all if you can't gather them?"

"What's the good of flowers when you *have* gathered them!" answered the Elf crossly. "They only fade. Much better leave them as they are."

But Miss Wide-awake would not be satisfied.

"Please, dear Elf, let me pick one—only a little one! I don't mind if it's quite a bud," she said.

The silver flowers bent gracefully towards her as if they were rather pleased, but the Elf looked very fierce.

"If you take my advice, you will leave them alone," he said.

It seemed, however, that the longer the

Elf refused to let her pick the flowers, the more Miss Wide-awake wished to do so.

"I must—indeed, I must have one!" she cried.

"Well, wait till to-morrow," replied the Elf; "there will be heaps of flowers that you can pick by daylight. The garden is full of them."

"But I like the moonflowers best of all."

"I wish I had never brought you," said the Elf, losing patience at last. "I had no idea you would go on like this."

"You *asked* me to come," returned Miss Wide-awake; "and you never told me I couldn't pick the moonflowers."

"No, I didn't say you couldn't, because I can't prevent you. You may gather them if you like; all I said was—*you had better not!*"

"Then I shall!" said Miss Wide-awake,

who had become very wilful; and stepping on the flower-bed, she reached up to pick the tallest and most beautiful of the moonflowers.

Just at that moment a strange thing happened. The moon, which had been calmly sailing overhead all this time, suddenly hid herself behind the branches of an old yew-tree, and at the very same moment the moonflowers vanished at Miss Wide-awake's touch.

At first she was very much puzzled, and when she looked round and saw how dark and gloomy the garden had become, she began to feel rather frightened and very much inclined to cry.

"There!" said the Elf. "I told you so!"

It was a little unkind of him to say that just when Miss Wide-awake was feeling so

SHE REACHED UP TO PICK THE TALLEST OF THE MOON-FLOWERS.

p. 18.

The Moon-Flowers.

sad, but even Elves like to prove that they are right sometimes.

"You didn't tell me so!" sobbed Miss Wide-awake, breaking down altogether.

"Well, don't let's argue about it," said the Elf. "It is time you were getting back to bed again."

Miss Wide-awake never knew how she got back to her little white cot, but the last thing she remembered was the Elf saying:

"You should leave things alone when you only see them by moonlight."

"Back to her little white cot."

CHAPTER III

FAIRY PAINTERS

"WHAT *are* you staring at?" asked the Elf one morning, when he found Miss Wide-awake sitting under the trees and gazing up through the branches, deep in thought.

"I was wondering," said she, "where all the colour comes from."

"Don't you know that? Why, I thought everybody knew about the Fairy Painters."

"Fairy Painters? I never even heard of them!"

"Well, that's strange, when you think what the world would look like if there weren't any."

"And do the Fairies really paint all the colours on the flowers and everything else?"

"Every bit of it. There isn't a scrap of a leaf or a flower that hasn't been painted by the Fairies. It makes them very busy, above all just now. Think of all the work that has to be done in the orchard alone. Pink and White have been at it quite a long time, and they have not finished yet. Each Fairy, you see, has its own colour, and paints everything that needs it. For instance, Pink and White paint all the apple-blossom and peach-blossom, a few roses, and the cheeks of all the babies in the world."

"Are you quite sure that the Fairies paint the babies' cheeks?" asked Miss Wide-awake.

"Quite sure. Just as people paint the dolls' faces, only the Fairies do it so much better that it won't wash off."

"I never thought of that before. Pink and White must be very busy Fairies."

"Oh yes; but not half so busy as Blue and Green. Blue, you see, has the whole sky to do, besides all the forget-me-nots and blue-bells. Sometimes he forgets to paint the sky, and then it looks dull and grey. Green does all the grass and trees and hedges. You can see him at work now. He has a wonderful way of making things smart, even when they look quite dingy and worn out. Then there's young Yellow. He's a very merry soul, and spends all his time touching up the dandelions and daffodils. Then the sunflowers and marigolds keep him busy until autumn, when he has to colour the cornfields. If you'd like to see Pink and White at their work, come along with me."

Miss Wide-awake followed the Elf until they came to the big apple-tree, and there, sure enough, on one of the lowest branches, two tiny fairy-men were busy with palette and brushes, tinting and colouring every bud and blossom as it opened to the sun.

"How happy they look!" said Miss Wide-awake, as she watched them fly from spray to spray.

"Yes," answered the Elf; "in this orchard you can only be happy if you are busy. Not that Pink and White have always been so; they once had a quarrel. It was about a rose. One wanted it to be a pink rose, and the other said it should be a white rose;

and as they could not agree, the end of it was they each painted a little bit of it, and so the rose was half pink and half white. But the quarrel did not end here, for one said it was a pink rose with white stripes, and the other would insist that it was a white rose with pink stripes, and they fought so fiercely over it that at last Pink said he would give up painting altogether, and White would have to do all the work alone.

"So that year there was no apple-blossom, and no pink may, nor could a single pink rose be found in all the world. Now, it happened that pink roses were the Fairy Queen's favourite flower, and when she was told that not one could be found in the whole country, she was much disappointed and annoyed. So she sent for Painter Pink to ask the reason why there were none

"Of course, Painter Pink had no answer to give, for it was his own hasty temper that had caused all the trouble.

"'Do you know what will happen if you neglect your work in this way?' asked the Fairy Queen. 'There will soon be no blossom and no fruit. I don't mind so much about the flowers, although I love pink roses best of all; but what about the roses in the cheeks of the little children? Are you going to let them suffer for your laziness?'

"Painter Pink began to look very much ashamed of himself.

"'I left it all for White to do,' he said.

"'Ah, yes,' said the Fairy Queen; 'but if White does it, they will have such pale faces everyone will think they are ill.'

"'I never thought of them at all,' said Painter Pink.

"'No, you were thinking only of yourself. Remember in future that whenever you leave your work undone, *someone* has to suffer for it. Now go and get your paints and brushes and make up for lost time.'

"So Painter Pink set to work again, and he has been busy ever since."

"It was horrid of him to forget the little children!" said Miss Wide-awake.

"Yes; but it is not always his fault when they have pale cheeks. He is good-natured enough, and works pretty hard as a rule; but he's rather a delicate little fellow, and there are some places where the air is so unhealthy and the streets so dark and narrow that he cannot work there at all, and so the children never have rosy faces. It's sad, of course, but one cannot blame him. Now with Green it's quite different. He's a much stronger chap, and there are very few places where he can't make himself at home. He told me once that he had discovered a plant growing in a dark cellar. It was a poor, sickly-looking thing, because it had never been out in the air and sunshine, and Green could not find his way into the cellar because the window was closely barred. However, he went every day to the place, hoping some time to find an entrance, for he knew that the poor plant must be longing to look smart and fresh like all other growing things. One day he asked Painter Pink to go with him, hoping that together they might find some way into the cellar; but when they came to the place, they found that the plant had been up-rooted and flung outside to wither.

"As it was still alive Pink and Green set to

work to tint and colour the slender stem with its frail leaves and pallid petals, and so tenderly and lovingly did they do it that the plant gained strength enough to revive and take root in the soil upon which it lay. Then it grew and thrived until it became a beautiful flowering tree which was admired by everyone who saw it."

"How very kind it was of Green!" said Miss Wide-awake. "I think I should like him the best of all the Fairy Painters."

"Oh yes," answered the Elf, "he's a great favourite. I've heard there's a country somewhere in the West where he is always so busy day and night that the whole land is called by his name."

"Is it?" asked Miss Wide-awake. "I don't think I ever heard of it."

"No, perhaps not," replied the Elf, with

his most learned air. "I should think there must be quite a lot of things *you* have never heard of, and places, too, to judge by your size. But I can't stop to tell you about it now . . ." and the Elf had flown away before Miss Wide-awake had time to ask another question.

"Hoping to find an entrance," p. 27.

CHAPTER IV

THE SECRET

THERE was no doubt about it—something unusual had taken place, but Miss Wide-awake had no idea what it was.

Yet everyone in the orchard was full of it; she knew that from the very first moment she entered by the little wooden gate.

It was a bright sunny morning, and everything seemed alive and joyous; but Miss Wide-awake felt quite certain that it was more than the sunshine which caused this flutter of excitement and set all the Birds a-singing in such a fashion. Then, too, the Bees were humming louder than usual, as if they were discussing something of great importance, and the Trees seemed to be whispering among themselves in hushed voices.

"I should like to know what it is all about," sighed Miss Wide-awake. "It must be something very interesting for them all to be making such a fuss. I'll ask the Elf when he comes—he's sure to know."

The Elf was rather later than usual in appearing, and when he did come it was easy to see that he knew all about it, for he looked excited and pleased.

Miss Wide-awake lost no time in asking for news.

"Tell me what has happened!" she said.

But the Elf pursed up his lips and looked very knowing.

"I can't tell you," he said ; "it's a secret."

"A secret !" echoed Miss Wide-awake. "Why, everyone in the orchard knows !"

"Of course; but that's because they've found out for themselves. Nobody has told them—it's against the rules."

Miss Wide-awake was very much put out; she had quite made up her mind to hear all about it from the Elf.

"What a stupid secret it must be !" she said. "A secret isn't a secret at all until somebody tells it to somebody else."

"In this orchard," replied the Elf very gravely, "a secret isn't a secret any longer when you have told it to anyone else—and most of all to a human being !"

"Well, never mind," said Miss Wide-awake,

brightening up a little. "Perhaps I can find out for myself if the others have done so."

"You can try if you like, but I don't think you will. You're not quite tall enough."

"Then I shall go and ask some of the others; perhaps they won't refuse to tell me."

The Elf chuckled to himself, and Miss Wide-awake walked away, feeling rather hurt.

"I'll go down to the brook," she said; "the frogs are very talkative, perhaps they will tell me."

But the frogs were too busy with their own affairs to pay any attention to Miss Wideawake, and though the rushes whispered a great deal among themselves, she could not understand a single word they said. Yet they all seemed to be talking about the same thing. Even the stream as it rippled past at her feet seemed to be singing about the secret, and Miss Wide-awake wished more than ever to know what it was.

Then she remembered that in the garden at the other side of the hedge she had seen the gardener bedding out plants. Now John the gardener was a very serious and thoughtful person, and Miss Wide-awake felt quite sure that if anybody knew about the secret *he* would; at any rate she would ask him.

So she hurriedly opened the little wooden gate and found John still busy among the geraniums. For a time she watched him in silence, wondering how she should begin; it was a little hard to explain what she had come for.

"John," she said at last, "have you heard any news this morning?"

John straightened himself up and looked

down at Miss Wide-awake with a very puzzled expression.

"News, Miss? No, I've heard nothing. Would it be something in the newspapers, Miss?"

"No, I don't think it would be in the papers, John; but I was wondering if you had noticed anything or found anything different from usual in the garden, or perhaps in the orchard?"

John rubbed his head.

"No, Miss, not that I know of. Have you lost something, Miss?"

"Oh no, John, I've not lost anything; but I thought perhaps you might have seen —it's a secret, you know."

"A secret, is it? Oh well, Miss, if I were you I'd let it alone. There's nothing to be gained from finding out secrets. It's better to let them as have them keep them."

With these words John wheeled his barrow away to the potting-shed, leaving Miss Wide-awake no wiser than she was before.

It was really very annoying, but there was nothing for it but to go back to the orchard again.

"I shan't find out much at this rate," grumbled Miss Wide-awake; "and it's just a waste of time stopping here. But I *do* want to know the secret!"

The sun was very hot just then, and when Miss Wide-awake reached the big apple-tree she flung herself down on the cool grass, feeling a little bit sleepy.

She had not been there very long before she heard voices in the boughs overhead. At first she thought it was a Blackbird singing in sweet, low notes to his mate, but the strange part of it was she could understand every word he said.

"She wants to know our secret," sang the Blackbird. "Did you hear her say so?"

"Yes, I'm quite sure she did. . . . Of course, it's rather dangerous; one never can trust people who live in real houses."

"But I think we might trust *her*. She looks quite kind and gentle now she's asleep."

"Then if you're quite *sure* she won't try to disturb them, or steal them, you may tell her."

"How many did you say there were?"

"Five, pale blue, with little brown specks on them."

"All right, I'll tell her. You're sure you don't mind?"

"Not a bit. I'm so proud and so happy, I want everyone to share our beautiful secret."

Then there was a flutter of wings, and suddenly the big Blackbird alighted on a lower bough, where he swung gaily to and fro, eyeing Miss Wide-awake in a knowing, friendly manner.

Having made quite sure that she must be harmless, because she looked so pretty and lay so still, he began to sing to her; and by-and-by he had poured out the whole secret right into Miss Wide-awake's ear.

It could not have been a dream, of course, because she had not been to sleep; and as soon as ever the Blackbird's song was ended, she sprang up from the grass and went in search of the Elf.

"I know! I know!" she cried, when she found him perched on a toadstool, which was his favourite seat.

"Well, what do you know?" inquired the Elf.

"Why, the secret," answered Miss Wide-awake.

"Have you seen them?" asked the Elf.

"No, I haven't seen them yet."

"Well, how did you find out, then?"

"Why, the Blackbirds told me themselves, said Miss Wide-awake.

* * * * *

Of course, *you* know what the secret was?

"The Blackbird alighted on a bough," p. 38.

CHAPTER V

THE FAIRY GARDEN

"TELL me more about the Fairy Garden," said Miss Wide-awake, who was now very friendly with the Elf. "Where is it, and how do you get there?"

"It is a long, long way from here," replied the Elf, "and I can't tell you how you get there. People have been there, of course, but no one ever seems to remember the way they went or how they got back again."

"Then tell me what it is like, because, you know, I *might* go some day!"

"Why, so you might," said the Elf; "and one thing is quite certain—you've never seen any place like it, for it's the loveliest spot in the world. You see, in the Fairy Garden the flowers bloom all the year round, and such wonderful flowers, too—not a bit like any that you see growing in the earth-garden; but then, you know, the Fairies take such care of them. They get all the sun and dew they need, and there are no rough storms to spoil their beauty, nor bitter frosts to nip their roots.

"The Fairies are very proud of their garden, and nothing is allowed to grow there that is not sweet and fair to see. Perhaps you have heard of some of the flowers that grow there. They call them 'Sweet Memories,' and 'Happy Thoughts,' but the sweetest and most beautiful of them all is the Love Plant, which grows and blossoms all over the garden.

"Now the Fairies are not selfish over their flowers as some earth-gardeners are, and sometimes they pick the blossoms and scatter them on the earth below. I have often seen people look quite surprised when a Fairy flower suddenly appears, and no one can tell where it comes from.

"It sometimes happens that no one sees them fall, and the careless people tread them under foot. This makes the Fairies very sad, for they love their flowers dearly, and grieve to see them injured or despised. Of course no earth-people are allowed to enter the garden, for though I have heard it said that everyone passes that way once in a lifetime, they only get a peep through the bars of the gate, and then pass on, forgetting all about it, because they have so many other things to remember.

"But one day it happened that a little Earth-Child came to the gate of the garden, and she did not pass on like the rest. For a time she stood looking longingly at the gay flowers and sunny walks, and watched the Fairies busy among the blossoms. Then, without knowing in the least how it happened, she suddenly opened the garden-gate and walked inside.

"What a strange, wonderful place it was! She had never seen anything half so beautiful before, but then you would not expect a Fairy Garden to be like any other place.

"The Fairies were very much upset when they saw the Earth-Child in the garden.

"'However did she get in here?' they cried; for it never occurred to them that the Earth-Child had opened the garden-gate herself.

"'Please don't be frightened,' said the Child; 'I won't do any harm. I came because it is winter-time on earth, and my own garden is dull and dreary. I have often heard of this garden, and I just came to see if it is as beautiful as people say.'

"'But you cannot stay here!' cried the Fairies in a chorus.

The Earth-Child looked very sad.

"'I have come a long, long way,' she said.

"'You must go back again,' said the Fairies.

"'But there are no flowers in the earth-gardens, and the winter is so long!'

"'You cannot stay here,' the Fairies replied.

"'You are too big,' said one.

"'You have no wings,' said another.

"'And the flowers would die if you touched them, because you are only an Earth-Child,' cried a third.

"It was quite useless to plead with the Fairies to let her stay, but it did seem hard to leave the lovely, sunny garden and go back to the dull, bare earth again. Indeed, there were tears in her eyes as the Earth-Child turned away, for if only the Fairies had allowed her to stay she might have been so happy there.

"It was quite plain that they were all very glad when she turned to go; but just before she passed through the garden-gate she heard a voice saying:

"'Stop! stop!'

"It was a Fairy who had followed the Earth-Child, and was holding out a tiny seed to her.

"'Take this,' said the Fairy, 'and plant it in your garden. It is a Fairy seed, but I think it will grow on earth if you tend it carefully; then you will have flowers all the year round.'

"The Earth-Child thanked the Fairy, and passed through the gate, feeling a little cheered by this kind act; and as soon as ever she reached the earth—she never quite knew how—she planted the seed in a sheltered corner of the garden.

"How eagerly the Earth-Child waited for the first signs of its growth! Every day she visited the place, and sometimes she feared that the seed would never take root in her garden.

"By-and-by, however, a tiny green blade appeared above the ground, and then she knew that her patient care was rewarded.

"So quickly did it grow that I think the Fairies themselves must have come secretly to tend it, or perhaps it was because of the love of the Earth-Child who watched it day by day. Strangers who came to the garden noticed the Fairy plant, because it was so unlike all the others. They said it was as rare as it was beautiful; but everyone called it by a different name, because they did not know the right one.

"The Earth-Child listened to them all, and smiled; she knew the right name, of course, but she never told anybody, although she heard it called as many as nine different names in one day!

"After a time the Fairy plant began to put

forth blossoms, and the Earth-Child remembered that the Fairy had told her she would have flowers all the year round.

" She soon found that this was quite true, and her heart was filled with great joy.

" Strange, beautiful flowers they were, too, for the more you gathered them, the more they bloomed, and the whole garden was filled with their scent. The strangers who came to the garden now went away with their hands full of blossoms, for the Earth-Child, who was almost grown up by this time, gave them away to all who cared to have them.

" ' Where did it come from, this wonderful plant ?' asked one.

" ' What is its name ?' cried another.

" ' How long have you had it ?' said a third.

"But the Earth-Child could answer none of these questions, for, to tell you the truth, she had quite forgotten all about her visit to the Fairy Garden, and could not tell how or when it came to be growing there.

"All she knew was, that the beautiful, fragrant flowers made herself and everyone else happy, for they blossomed all the year round, and, for all I know, they are blossoming still!"

CHAPTER VI

THE SUNDIAL

THE Sundial stood on a grassy mound in one corner of the garden. Miss Wide-awake could only reach the top of it by standing on tiptoe, and she often wondered what it was for, and who had put it there, for it was rather a queer-looking thing. She thought, too, that it must be very old, because the stonework was crumbling away—indeed, it looked as if it had stood there since the beginning of the world.

"Old! I should think it *is* old!" said the Elf one day, as he sat on the edge of the Dial, swinging his legs over the side.

He always seemed to know exactly what Miss Wide-awake was thinking about.

"Older than the Apple-Tree?" she asked.

"Oh, much, much older. I shouldn't like to say how old."

"But is it any *use?*"

"Why, of course. It counts all the minutes and hours as they pass."

"But what is the good of counting them?"

"To prevent them being lost, to be sure."

Miss Wide-awake looked very puzzled, so the Elf went on to explain.

"You see, the Sundial has to make sure that each day has just the right number of minutes and hours. It's very difficult at times because, you know, they are always getting lost, and if it were not for the Sun the poor old Dial would get in a terrible muddle sometimes."

"How do they get lost?" asked Miss Wide-awake.

"It's never the Sundial's fault, poor thing, it always does its very best to take care of them. The Hours and Minutes come sliding down the Sunbeams, you know. Some are swift and shining, and others slow and sad, but they all fall in turn upon the Sundial, and leave a kiss upon its old wrinkled face—all except those that get lost, and it's always somebody's fault if it's only a Minute that's missing. . . . A whole Hour was lost yesterday."

"Who lost it?" asked Miss Wide-awake.

"Why, *you* did!"

"I didn't know I had."

"No, very often people don't know when they lose the Hours—at least, not till a long time afterwards."

"But what becomes of them?"

"Ah! that's what everybody wants to know, but no one has found out yet. You'd never guess where all the lost hours are!"

"Then please tell me, dear Elf."

"I won't *tell* you—I'll take you there!" said the Elf, with surprising good humour.

"Is it far?" inquired Miss Wide-awake.

"Oh no; you'll be there almost directly. Just follow me."

While he was speaking the Elf jumped lightly down from his seat and pointed to a tiny opening at the foot of the Sundial. At first it seemed to be nothing but a crevice in the stonework, but, when she looked at it more closely, she saw that it was really a doorway, and by bending her head a little she was able to enter it after the Elf.

They found themselves in a long passage, which was rather dark and chilly, but presently this opened into a big silent hall which was filled with strange, shadowy forms.

"There are the Lost Hours," said the Elf, "and those little things trooping in at the door are the Minutes."

"How unhappy they look!" whispered Miss Wide-awake.

"Of course they do," replied the Elf; "they all want to be out in the sunshine instead of being imprisoned in this dreary place."

"Will they ever get out again?"

"Oh yes, some of them may in time, if

the people who lost them set about finding them again in the right way. They call it 'making up for lost time,' you know, and it means working ever so much harder than you ever did before. The Minutes have the best of it; they often get out because people don't mind hard work for a minute or two. But when it comes to the Hours and Days, it's quite a different thing; they are often shut up here for years, because no one will take the trouble to set them free."

"It isn't a bit fair——" began Miss Wide-awake, and then suddenly stopped short, looking very red and confused, for there, face to face with her, was one of her own Lost Hours!

"Yes," it said in a tired voice, looking sadly at Miss Wide-awake, "I am the Hour you lost yesterday over your lessons.

You *would* sit and stare out of the window instead of doing your sums, and although it was such a beautiful day, and I longed to be out in the garden, I had to leave the fresh air and sunshine, and come into this dismal place. Worst of all, I could not even kiss the dear old Sundial, because I am a Lost Hour and must stay here."

"I am very sorry," said Miss Wide-awake, feeling very guilty.

"Being sorry won't do any good," grumbled the Lost Hour.

"What must I do, then?"

"Why, every day you must work a little harder than you did the day before, and then some day, perhaps, you will have made up for the time you lost yesterday, and I shall get out of this hateful place."

Miss Wide-awake promised to do this very

"I AM THE HOUR YOU LOST YESTERDAY."

willingly, for she was really sorry to think that her own laziness had made a prisoner of the Hour.

"I never knew anything about Lost Hours before," she said, as she followed the Elf back to the garden again. "I used to wonder what the Sundial was for, but I never thought all the Lost Hours were *inside* it!"

"Well, now you know, I should think you would try not to send any more in there," said the Elf.

"I shall try not to, of course," said Miss Wide-awake; and quite suddenly she found herself sitting on the grassy mound alone, for the Elf was nowhere to be seen.

But the old Sundial was looking just the same as usual!

CHAPTER VII

THE CHERRY-TREE

"DO you see that cherry-tree over there?" asked the Elf. "Well, don't appear to be looking at it, and I'll tell you its story.

It's really a stranger, you know, and doesn't belong to the orchard at all. I'll tell you how it got here.

Far away in a distant part of the ocean

there lies a beautiful island, where the sun shines all the year round, and the grass is as green as the seas are blue.

The island is covered with wonderful flowering trees and shrubs of many different kinds; but most wonderful of all are the cherry-trees, which grow there in such quantities that men have called it the "Land of Cherry-Blossom." Long before a ship reaches the shores of the island the perfume of the cherry-blossom is wafted across the water by the soft winds, and the sailors call it their first welcome home.

The people of the island are happy and contented, as, indeed, they ought to be in such a lovely spot; they never wish to wander far from their home, but they are always kind and friendly to the strangers who land upon their shores.

Years and years ago it happened that a Traveller from the West came to the island and was greatly struck by its beauty. So much so, indeed, that he chose to remain there for some time, and the people took great pride and pleasure in showing him all the wonders of the place.

One day, as the Traveller wandered about among the fragrant avenues of cherry-trees, he suddenly came across a little lady seated in a shady spot. Her skin was as white as the blossom overhead, and her lips as red as cherries themselves; the Traveller thought her quite the most beautiful sight in the whole island.

The next day he walked the same way again, and the little lady raised her eyes and smiled at him as he passed. On the third day he found her sitting there as usual, and he thought he would speak a few polite words to her, pretending to admire the cherry-trees, while all the time he was really admiring her.

So they talked together for many days, until the Traveller had almost forgotten that there were other lands to visit.

"There cannot be any place in the world so beautiful as this," he said one day to the little lady.

"Is not your own country more beautiful?" she asked.

"It is the best country in the world!" answered the Traveller.

"Tell me all about it," said the little lady; and the Traveller fell to describing the woods and fields and towns and villages of his home in the West, and at the end of it all he asked little Cherry-Blossom if she would go back with him to that distant country.

The little lady looked surprised and sad.

"Ah, no," she said, "I cannot come."

The Traveller begged hard. "You shall have everything you wish for," he said.

But Cherry-Blossom only shook her head and answered: "Indeed, I cannot come."

"But why will you not come?"

"Because in your country there are no cherry-trees!"

Now this was perfectly true, for in all his life the Traveller could not remember ever having seen a cherry-tree before he came to the island.

At last the time came to say good-bye, but before he went away the Traveller asked Cherry-Blossom for a keepsake.

"What is a keepsake?" asked the little lady.

"Something to remember your friends by," answered the Traveller.

"But I have nothing—nothing in the world to give you," said Cherry-Blossom.

"Give me—a cherry-stone! It is all I want," said the Traveller; and the little lady laughed merrily as she felt deep in her pocket and found a cherry-stone, which she gave him as they said farewell.

After many months the Traveller returned to his home in the West, and the first thing he did was to plant the cherry-stone in the garden near his house, thinking all the time of the distant island and the little lady he had left behind.

It was several years before a cherry-tree grew up, but the Traveller watched it patiently all the time; and when at last it had reached the height of the door-post, he set out again and sailed across the sea to the island.

He found Cherry-Blossom seated under the trees, just as if she had been waiting there for him all the time.

"Will you come back to my home with me?" asked the Traveller. "There is a cherry-tree in my front garden."

"Only *one?*" said the little lady. "Here there are nothing but cherry-trees. I could never be satisfied with only one!"

The Traveller turned away with a very sad heart. He had waited so long for that one tree to grow; it seemed hard that it should not be enough.

However, before he left the island, he filled his pockets full of cherry-stones; and when he got back to his home in the West he planted them in his garden and watched and waited for them to grow.

By-and-by they sprouted and shot up into

tall, slender trees, until there were quite a number of them budding and blossoming round his house. Then, proud and pleased, he sailed away to the island once more, and found the little lady waiting for him as before.

"There is a whole orchard of cherry-trees round my house—will you come back with me now?" he asked.

But the little lady shook her head.

"I cannot come," she said, "until the whole country is covered with cherry-trees."

So the Traveller went home again, grieved but still hopeful, with a shipload of cherry-stones, and he spent his whole life wandering up and down the country, planting them here, there, and everywhere, hoping that in time there would be quite enough cherry-trees to please even the little lady in the distant island.

As the years went by, the Traveller became an old man, but he never gave up his task, and wherever he went a cherry-tree sprang up in his steps. Every spring, when the orchard-trees burst into bloom, he said to himself, "She is sure to come this year!"

But the little lady must have forgotten all about the Traveller and his home in the West, for she has not come yet.

* * * * *

Perhaps there are not enough cherry-trees!

"Seated in a shady spot," p. 60.

CHAPTER VIII

THE APPLE-TREE'S STORY

"I AM really very old," said the Apple-Tree, "though you might not think so from my appearance to-day. I can remember things that happened ever so long ago, when the Pear-Tree over there was no higher than the hedge, and I can tell you many a story about what I have seen and heard in this orchard. Perhaps you wouldn't think there was much going on here, even at the best of times, but it's really wonderful how much you get to know if you only live long enough. The story I am going to tell you is a very old one, but I don't see that it is any the worse for that."

There was once a little girl just like you, Miss Wide-awake, who used to come and play in the orchard every day. She was a lonely little person, and though she had not half so many dolls as you, she never seemed to want them, for she had a wonderful way of making up games by herself, and talking aloud, as if she were half a dozen people all rolled into one! She came, of course, from the big house you live in. I used to be able to see it quite plainly through the trees, but now I can only catch a glimpse of the chimneys in winter when the leaves have fallen.

My little lady never spoke of brothers or sisters, so I suppose she was an only child, like you, Miss Wide-awake. Her games were mostly about brave knights and noble ladies, secret hiding-places and fierce fighting, and, indeed, to hear her talk sometimes, you could almost imagine that the orchard was full of armed men!

It seemed that her father was a soldier, and if he did one-half the brave and splendid things his little daughter believed he did, he must have been a very brave man indeed.

Sometimes my little lady would bring a story-book, and read aloud about giants and witches, and princes and princesses. Such wonderful stories they were! Her cheeks grew pink and her eyes brightened as she read them ; then she would sit at my feet for hours together, making up pretty stories of her own, which were even more wonderful than those in the book.

But by-and-by there came a sort of sadness into her day-dreams ; she seemed to wish for something beyond the orchard, and I often saw her standing by the hedge and gazing down the high-road, as if she were looking out for something or somebody, and half expected them to come that way.

I often used to wonder what she was looking for. It seemed rather a waste of time to stand there bending forward her head to watch for somebody who never came. But one day I found out all about it.

My little lady came stepping into the orchard one morning with a step as light as a fairy, and talking to herself, as she always did when she was happy.

"He is *sure* to come to-day," she said, throwing herself down on the grass at my feet. "It's the Prince, you know; they say he is sure to pass this way. He will come riding along the high-road, and you are quite certain to see him if you only wait long enough. He wears a suit of dazzling armour, and rides a beautiful white horse. Oh, I hope he will come to-day!"

I had never seen anyone like that riding along the high-road; they were mostly farmers and huntsmen who passed that way. But, of course, I believed my lady when she said the Prince was coming. She read a great many story-books, you see, so I felt sure she must know all about it.

Well, I held up my branches as high as

I could, which was rather difficult, because the fruit was forming, and this made them very heavy, and we watched most of the day, my little lady and I, but no one passed who was at all like the Prince.

A farm-boy with some sheep went by, and the stage-coach from the neighbouring town rattled past with a great cloud of dust behind it, but never a horseman of any kind did we see, and I felt sure my lady must be sadly disappointed.

"Never mind!" I heard her say, as if she were trying to comfort someone else. "Perhaps he will come to-morrow," and then it was time for her to go home.

I quite expected to see her the next day, but she did not come, and not for many, many days after. Indeed, seven summers passed before my lady came again to the orchard.

She was quite grown up by that time, and very much changed—I think she had been away from home—but I'm sure I should have known her anywhere. She had a letter in her hand which she read over many times, just as she used to read the story-books in the old days.

Then she began to talk to herself in the same old childish way.

"Perhaps he will come to-day," she said. "I will stand by the hedge, and then I shall see him coming from far off, and I can wave to him to show that I am waiting."

So she stood once more looking over the hedge, with her handkerchief in her hand, expecting someone to come along the high-road.

I suppose it was the Prince again, so I looked out too, and waved my topmost branches whenever I saw anyone coming down the road.

But when they came nearer we saw that it was not the Prince after all; only just a labourer from the farm down the road, or a traveller journeying to the next town. So my lady still waited for her Prince after seven summers had come and gone, and she seemed just as certain that he would come—if she only waited long enough.

The fruit ripened early that year, and a magnificent show my rosy-cheeked apples made when they gathered them and took them away to the big house. After that the leaves began to fall; then came stormy weather, and the rough wind tore away some of my branches, and left them to rot upon the ground.

I was very much surprised to see my lady walking in the orchard on a wet, windy day in the late autumn. She looked very sad and lonely, and I fancied there were tear-stains on her face. She seemed to forget, too, that it was no longer summer, for she came and stood under my bare branches, and leaned her head against my rough, old trunk.

"He will never come now," she whispered. "I don't think he will ever come now."

I had never heard such sad words before, and my old heart cracked with pain when I felt her hot tears falling on my moss-grown bark. It seemed a very long winter, and all the surrounding country lay half buried in snow, and I never saw my lady again for several months.

But when the snow melted and the roads

could be used again, I noticed that more people than usual were going along the road towards the big house, and it seemed as if something out of the common were about to take place.

Then one day I overheard two passers-by talking on the other side of the hedge. They spoke of a wedding, and I heard my lady's name mentioned more than once, so of course I listened with great care.

It was now getting on towards spring, and all the fruit-trees were ready to bud out. The orchard had long been left alone, until one day my lady came again, and I could not help seeing how happy she looked and how joyous her voice sounded, just like some bird singing to its mate. This time she never looked over the hedge at all, she simply danced over the grass, plucked a bunch of daffodils to wear at her waist, and went away still singing to herself. It was all very strange; she had never behaved quite like this before.

A short time after this we heard the church bells ringing a joyous peal, and a great many carriages dashed up the road towards the big house and back again. The Pear-Tree, having grown very tall, announced that a flag was flying over the house. Certainly something very stirring was taking place, and, not to be outdone by the bells and the sunshine, we all hastened to deck ourselves for the occasion, and I don't think there was ever such a show of blossom before.

And, looking back, it could only mean one thing—the Prince had come!

* * * * *

You may think you have heard this story before, or something very like it, and perhaps you have.

There is nothing new under the sun, so the story-books say.

"The road to the big house," p. 76.

CHAPTER IX

THE CROCUSES

"STOP!" cried the Elf; "you are walking on their heads!"

Miss Wide-awake stepped hastily aside. She was wandering over the grass beneath the big Copper-Beech-Tree one bright spring morning, when she was suddenly startled by hearing the Elf's angry cry.

"You really must be more careful," he went on; "nobody likes being trodden upon."

"But I didn't know I was treading on anybody," said Miss Wide-awake.

"Oh, that often happens," replied the Elf. "You would think some people were quite blind the way they go blundering about and trampling others beneath their feet!"

Poor little Miss Wide-awake felt very uncomfortable indeed; it was not nice to be called blind and blundering when you didn't know you had been doing any harm.

"But I don't see anyone even now," she said.

"Then you must be *really* blind! What a pity! Or perhaps it's because your head is so far away from your feet!"

Miss Wide-awake glanced down at her feet at these words, and there for the first time she saw quantities of tiny green spikes peeping up through the grass, and at the same time she heard a faint murmur of voices which seemed to come right out of the ground.

"It's the Crocuses," said the Elf; "they are getting ready for their ball."

"A ball? How lovely! Oh, when is it to be?"

"As soon as the Sunbeams have sent all the invitations out. It takes a long time. Every single Crocus gets one, and there are hundreds of them in this garden alone."

"Oh, how I wish they would bring *me* one!" exclaimed Miss Wide-awake, forgetting for the moment that she was only a little girl and not a Crocus.

"I might manage it for you," said the Elf, looking important; "but I don't know what you would do about a dress."

"What sort of dress should I need?" asked Miss Wide-awake, getting very excited.

"Well, you see, the Crocuses make their own. That's why they are so busy now. You can hear them quite plainly if you listen; they are trying to decide what colour to wear. It's very difficult for them, because they must be either purple or white or yellow."

"I've got a white party frock, if that would do. Oh, *dear* Elf, do you think the Sunbeams will bring me an invitation?"

"They *might*," replied the Elf; "I can't promise it. But you had better go home now and see what happens. It might come at any moment, and it would be a pity if you were not there to receive it."

For the next few days Miss Wide-awake was looking forward eagerly. It was beautiful spring weather; the bright sunshine shone over everything, and playful breezes stirred the budding trees. It seemed to Miss Wide-awake that the grass was greener and the sky bluer than she had ever seen them before. Very anxiously she watched and waited for some sign or message from the Crocuses, but it was not until several days later that her wish was granted. She was lying asleep in her little white bed when an Early Morning Sunbeam found its way through the window and fell across her face. She felt something like a soft, warm kiss upon her cheek, and opening her eyes wide she saw the words:

"*You are invited to the Crocuses' Ball*"

dancing before her in letters of purple and gold.

"Oh, thank you! thank you!" cried Miss Wide-awake in the wildest delight; but almost as she spoke the Sunbeam vanished and the gold and purple message faded from her sight.

Jumping out of bed, she dressed in great haste, and went out to find the Elf. He was brushing his hair beneath a laurel bush, and she was not in the least surprised when she found out that he had heard the news already.

"So you've got the invitation?" he said.

"Yes, the Sunbeams brought it this morning, just when I was waking up; but they didn't stay a moment, and I don't know when or where the ball will be."

"On the lawn, under the Copper-Beech-Tree, very early to-morrow morning; so mind you are there. Some of the guests have arrived already. I saw quite a lot as I passed that way an hour ago; but I can't waste any more time talking now, as I have to go and get a new suit of clothes for myself. The Crocuses dress so smartly, I couldn't go in this old coat."

* * * * *

Miss Wide-awake had meant to wake very early next morning, but even before she opened her eyes she heard a gentle tapping at the window, and the Elf's voice calling her name.

She feared very much that something must be wrong, and sprang hastily out of bed to let him in.

Alas! it was only too true. The window-panes were splashed with rain, and it was a very wet and draggled little figure that crept in and stood shivering on the window-sill.

"I came to tell you that something dreadful has happened," he said, in a miserable voice. "There isn't going to be any ball

. . . the sparrows have pecked off all the yellow Crocuses!"

Miss Wide-awake was very unhappy at this news.

"I didn't know birds *could* be so wicked!" she said.

"It's all greediness!" replied the Elf sadly. "They have nothing nice to eat just now, because all the berries are gone and the fruit is not ready . . . and yellow Crocuses are very good—so they say. . . . Oh, it *is* sad to see them lying on the ground, and all the other Crocuses grieving for them. They are quite broken-hearted."

It was a sad day for everyone in the garden. The rain fell pitilessly, and Miss Wide-awake sat at the nursery window gazing out upon the wet grass and dripping trees. Overhead she could hear the naughty sparrows chirping in the eaves; they always seemed to be quarrelling.

"If only the rain would stop," she said, "I would go out into the garden and gather all the yellow Crocuses that are left. They would be quite safe in water in my little blue bowl."

Later on the rain ceased and a watery sun appeared, and Miss Wide-awake lost no time in hurrying out into the garden. She went straight to the old Copper-Beech-Tree, where the grass was carpeted with Crocuses, but, alas! all the yellow ones were lying broken upon the ground, their bright petals torn and scattered in all directions.

Forgetting all about the damp grass, Miss Wide-awake knelt down among them, and gathered the broken flowers gently in her hands.

"Oh, you poor, poor little flowers!" she said, "I am so sorry for you!" and her hot tears fell upon the grass.

And suddenly it seemed as if other voices in the garden repeated her words. A bumblebee hummed them softly, as he flew from one flower to another, the wind in the laurel-bushes whispered them to the rustling leaves, while a thrush perched in the Copper-Beech-Tree made them into a song so tender and sweet that even the naughty sparrows were touched, and began to feel sorry for their wrongdoing.

"I don't think it will happen again," said the Elf, who had been looking on at a little distance. "I heard the sparrows saying they were sorry. If you would strew a few crumbs for them all the year round perhaps they would not try to eat your flowers. At least, I am told so by the lady of another beautiful garden where I go. She feeds the little birds all the year round, and they never touch her Crocuses."

By this time Miss Wide-awake had collected all the golden petals, so that no trace of the sad havoc remained. So intent was she upon her task that she never noticed that wherever she trod another Crocus bloomed to take the place of those which the sparrows had broken off, and the grown-up people said the Crocuses were more beautiful that year than they had ever been before.

Perhaps the Elf had something to do with it.

CHAPTER X

THE WASP'S STORY

"ARE you afraid of Wasps?" asked the Elf one day, when he and Miss Wide-awake were sitting under a plum-tree laden with ripe plums.

"Ye-es," replied Miss Wide-awake, feeling a little ashamed of herself.

"I don't see why you should be," said the Elf; "they don't mean any harm."

"But they do sting!" retorted Miss Wide-awake.

"So do you sometimes—with your tongue. Everybody does, very often without knowing it, and it hurts more than Wasps' stings. Then there's more excuse for Wasps, for they never have any kindness shown to them. . . . A Wasp once told me no one had ever been kind to him in his life. He was a handsome fellow, too."

"But why was everyone unkind to him?"

"Well, perhaps I had better tell you his story, and then you can judge for yourself."

So Miss Wide-awake settled herself comfortably in the long grass, feeling very drowsy, while the Wasps buzzed among the ripe plums overhead, and the Elf repeated this story:

As I have said, he was a very fine fellow, and he wore a bright yellow waistcoat, picked out with black, which made his waist look trim and slender. He began life in this orchard. His mother was one of the handsomest Queen Wasps that was ever seen, and she and her very large family made a nest in a sandy part of the bank under the hedge which separates the orchard from the road. There they all lived very happily until one day John the Gardener discovered the nest, and decided that it must be destroyed. I never could understand why, but Real People often do things which we Garden Folk cannot understand.

John the Gardener got Jim the Stable-boy to help him, and together they made a great fire and smoke under the hedge where the nest was, and all the poor Wasps flew out in dreadful distress.

I have never seen so much trouble in this orchard before. It is generally a very peaceful place, but that day it seemed as if it could never be the same again. Thick clouds of smoke rose in the air, all the birds and butterflies flew wildly away in terror, while the Wasps swarmed round about, watching their home perish among the flames. No wonder they grew angry and revengeful. I, for one, do not blame them, and some of the braver ones among them actually settled on John the Gardener and Jim the Stable-boy and stung them in several places. It was all they could do, poor things ! Many of them died afterwards, but among those who escaped was the young Wasp with the bright yellow waistcoat, and he flew over the hedge and out into the wide world beyond, vowing to himself that men and boys were his enemies for ever.

He found the world a pleasant place enough, for there were fields and gardens and a wide moorland covered with heather, where he spent many happy hours sucking honey from the heather-bells, which tasted even sweeter than that of the blossoms in the orchard.

But just at the height of his enjoyment he happened to meet a little brown Bee, who was also busy gathering honey from the heather-bells.

The young Wasp bowed politely to her and wished her "Good-morning."

"Don't interrupt me!" replied the little Bee crossly; "I've no time to spare talking to you!"

The young Wasp felt somewhat hurt.

"But I am gathering honey from the

heather, too," he said, "and I thought it would be pleasant to work together."

The little brown Bee buzzed angrily.

"What! I work with *you*—a selfish, greedy Wasp, who only sucks honey for himself, and has no respectable hive to go home to! Why, the other Bees would be furious if they saw me even speaking to you!"

Bitterly hurt by these words, the young Wasp turned away. It was not his fault that he had no home to go to, and, after all, in his family he had never been taught to gather honey for someone else, for he had work of another kind to do.

Sad at heart, he left the pleasant moorland and the sweet heather, and flew away and away until he came to a village on a hillside where the windows of a cottage stood open as if asking him to enter, and a delicious scent of something good to eat made him feel very hungry. Within the cottage a kindly-looking woman was working at a table, and without a thought of danger the young Wasp buzzed around her and at last alighted on the very dish she was using. Instantly her kind expression changed to one of wrath.

"Nasty, greedy creature!" she said; and seizing a cloth which was close at hand, she struck out angrily at the poor Wasp, who only just managed to escape the blow.

He flew towards the window, but in his blind fear he could not tell which was the open pane, and so beat himself madly against the glass in his efforts to find a way out.

Bruised and terrified, at last he found himself in the open air, and he flew for a long distance without stopping. It really seemed as if all living creatures were his enemies, although he had never done any harm to anyone!

His next adventure was in a sunny garden, where a number of children were having tea upon the lawn. They all looked so happy and gay that the young Wasp felt sure *they* would be kind to him, so he joined the jolly party, buzzing in sheer delight at finding himself among them.

Alas! his appearance caused the greatest terror and dismay; some of the children screamed, some flicked at him with handkerchiefs, while others ran away.

"Let him settle on the jam!" cried one, "then we can kill him!"

But the cruel words were scarcely spoken before the Wasp, now really angry, settled on the boy's face and drove his sting sharply in.

"Horrid, cruel wasp!" the child shrieked out in pain; and in the uproar which followed the Wasp flew over the garden-wall and away, feeling more sad than ever.

It was the first time he had ever stung anyone, and he felt as if he had behaved badly. But the children were really most to blame, for the young Wasp had not meant to hurt anyone when he joined their happy party.

Weak and weary from his long flight, he stopped at last in a sweet shady place that seemed strangely familiar. It was, in fact, his old home, the Orchard, and very quiet and restful it seemed to the poor tired Wasp.

The dusk was gathering, and the only living creature he could see was a little White Lady Moth, who was fluttering about in the shade.

"What is the matter?" she asked gently,

when she saw the Wasp lying quite worn out on the ground.

"I am very unhappy," replied the Wasp, "for I have travelled a long, long way, and you are the first person who has spoken kindly to me."

The little Lady Moth drew nearer and fanned him softly with her white wings.

"I have often heard that the world is a very cruel place," she said.

"But I must be very wicked," said the Wasp, "for everybody seems to hate me."

"I have also heard," replied the Moth, "that no one is so bad that they have not any good in them."

"But I am selfish and greedy and cruel," said the Wasp. "At least, so human creatures say."

"At any rate you are honest, and that

counts for a great deal," said the kind little Moth, and the Wasp's heart grew quite glad at the words.

"I do believe," he said, "if someone would be kind to me I should be a much better fellow than I am!"

"Dear Wasp, I don't think you *can* be so wicked," whispered the Moth; and the end of it was that the ill-treated Wasp and the little Lady Moth became great friends, and lived near each other here in the old Orchard for many happy days

* * * * *

"Oh!" said Miss Wide-awake, "I *am* glad he was happy at last, and I will try not to be afraid of Wasps any more."

"That's right," said the Elf, "always try to believe the best of people—and Wasps—even if you are sometimes mistaken. . . .

And remember, if you don't attack a Wasp first, he will not be in the least likely to hurt you, even if he does buzz round in rather a noisy fashion. See! there is a ripe plum fallen on the ground. Wouldn't you like to eat it?"

And Miss Wide-awake did.

"*Happy days*," p. 100.

CHAPTER XI

LADY LAVENDER

"I'M expecting a friend of mine this afternoon," said the Elf; "she generally visits this garden about this time of year, and I should like you to meet her."

"Who is she?" asked Miss Wide-awake.

"Her name is Lady Lavender. She belongs to a very old family which has bloomed in the best gardens for years. She herself is a little old-fashioned, perhaps, but everybody loves her, for when she is near, her sweet scent reminds people of happy, bygone days; old folk remember places they knew when they were children—gardens they played in and homes they loved. The way she has of bringing back the past is almost like magic. . . . She can tell you lots of stories, too."

"I wish she would come," said Miss Wide-awake. "I would like to hear one of her stories."

Just as she spoke a tiny figure in a faded, blue dress appeared, and the air was filled with the sweetest scent.

"Here I am!" said the little lady. "I've just called in to get a fresh supply of perfume from the Lavender bed near the south wall. My busy time is just beginning, you see, and I knew I should find plenty here. Did someone say she wanted to hear one of my stories? I haven't much time to spare, but I can tell you one which is quite, quite true," and, seating herself daintily upon the grass between the Elf and Miss Wide-awake, the little lady began her tale:

Far from here in the North Country there is a sweet old-fashioned garden which I visit every year, and it is always full of fragrant old-world blossoms such as your grandmother loved, my dear, when she was a girl.

Thyme and Lad's Love, Pinks and Sweet William, Gilly-Flowers and Pansies, grow there in a delicious tangle, but the flower that flourishes best of all is Sweet Lavender.

The Lady of the Garden loved it more than any other flower, and in summer-time she spent many hours gathering the sprigs and making them into fragrant bunches tied with dainty ribbons. She sent the bunches away to people in distant places, and each bunch carried a message from the Lady of the Garden.

While her fingers were busy with the flowers a little fair-haired boy played at her side. He knew nothing of the big world beyond the gates, and he was always happy playing in the old-fashioned garden.

Often his mother would join him in his games, and sometimes she would sing this quaint old rhyme to him as she sat at her work :

> " Lavender's blue, diddle, diddle,
> Lavender's green ;
> When I am King, diddle, diddle,
> You shall be Queen !"

Ah, what a happy little boy he was, and how swiftly the days passed in that pleasant garden !

But by-and-by he grew into a big boy, and the time came for him to go to school, leaving his mother alone.

Of course he came back for the holidays, and he always found her waiting for him with happy smiles and loving words; but somehow the garden did not seem so large or so interesting as it used to do, and he found more pleasure now in the world outside.

Years passed away and the boy grew into a man. He was tall and strong and clever, and he lived in a large city and worked hard all day long until he grew very rich and was admired and respected by everyone. But he was always so busy now that he had no time to go back to the old garden in the

North Country, for it was a long, long journey, and his work was so great that he hardly ever thought of his mother, who waited and longed for him, and sang the old rhyme to herself as she gathered the Lavender and tied it into bunches. Now, by a strange chance, it happened that some of these bunches of Lavender found their way into the hands of a poor girl who stood at the corner of a street in the great city and sold flowers to the passers-by.

But among all the hurrying throngs of people there were very few who had time to stop and buy, though the scent of the Lavender reached them as they passed and brought back to mind some sweet memory of bygone days, so that for a few brief moments they forgot their troubles and sorrows, and felt happy and young again.

One day the busy man passed by the corner of the street where the girl was selling Lavender. His mind was full of the great work he was doing and the riches and fame it would bring him.

Quite suddenly the faint, sweet scent of the Lavender was wafted in his face, and all at once the crowded street faded from his view, and he saw instead the old garden in the North Country, and his mother, old and grey-haired, waiting patiently for the son who never came.

No wonder he forgot the great work he was doing and turned instead to buy all that was left of the Lavender from the girl at the street corner, little thinking that his mother's frail fingers had tied up the bunches.

He sat for hours in his office that day

trying to fix his mind upon his work, but all in vain; and then he fell asleep and dreamed that he was a little fair-haired boy again, playing in the old garden at his mother's side, and he heard her voice singing the old rhyme:

"Lavender's blue, diddle, diddle,
Lavender's green;
When I am King, diddle, diddle,
You shall be Queen!"

This was the message which the Lavender had brought him, and in a few short hours he was travelling swiftly towards the North, leaving the crowded city and all the riches and fame he had hoped for far behind.

* * * * *

In the glow ot a summer evening he reached his old home and stood lingering at the gate, almost fearing to enter the garden he had loved as a child.

Then the scent of the sprig of Lavender which he wore in his buttonhole bade him take courage, and spoke of the mother who waited and longed for him within. And there, at last, he found her under the shadow of the fir-trees, old and frail now, but tender and loving still, as she had always been.

It was a joyous meeting, for both felt that the old, happy days had come back again, and, as they sat hand in hand in the peaceful garden, he showed her the sprig of Lavender which he wore in his buttonhole, and told her of the message it had brought him.

* * * * *

"So you see," said Lady Lavender, "even a little flower has its use."

"It's a lovely story!" said Miss Wide-awake;

"but I would like to know if he ever went back to the city again?"

But there was no answer to this question, because Lady Lavender had flown away!

"*The old garden*," p. 108.

CHAPTER XII

THE QUARRELSOME ROOKS

"CAW! Caw! Caw!" called the Rooks high up in the Elm-Tree, with shrill and noisy voices.

"What *is* the matter with them?" asked Miss Wide-awake; "they always seem to be unhappy or quarrelling about something."

"Yes, they are quarrelsome folk," said the

Elf. "I once climbed up into the Elm-Tree to find out what it was all about."

"And did you hear what it was?"

"Well," replied the Elf, "there seemed to be so many things they could not agree about. There was one young couple especially who fell out over everything.

"First of all they could not decide where their nest should be built, because one wanted it to be in the tallest Elm-Tree, and the other thought the old sycamore was the best building site. They argued so long and so fiercely about it that the nest never got started at all that day. It was Sunday morning, too, the first Sunday in March, which is the day that Rooks always choose to begin building their nests, so I have heard.

"When the place was chosen at last in the tallest Elm-Tree a fresh quarrel arose about how it should be built and what it should be made of. Mrs. Rook wanted it to be soft and warm, and Mr. Rook preferred it stout and strong, which really was more sensible when you think of the high winds which rock the tree-tops even in the summer-time.

"However, between them they managed to build a very snug little home ready for the Baby Rooks that were coming. But Mr. Rook found fault with the house-keeping, and Mrs. Rook complained of his neglect when he went out to get a good meal, so that there was never a day without a dispute of some kind.

"Then they began to fall out with their neighbours in the Rookery. There was a good deal of ill-natured gossip about the newcomers, and some of the old birds made spiteful remarks about young Mrs. Rook.

"How they wrangled, to be sure! It really was sad to hear the way they went on, calling each other names, and saying all the most unkind things they could think of.

"One would have thought that when the Baby Rooks arrived things might have improved, but Mr. Rook had grown selfish, and went off amusing himself all day, while Mrs. Rook stayed at home and grumbled. When the Baby Rooks were hatched, matters grew even worse, for there was hardly any room in the nest, and Father Rook was always kept outside.

"The poor babies were very much overcrowded, and the younger ones were almost crushed to death by the older and stronger birds.

"When they were fledged a very sad thing happened. It was a chilly night in May, with a touch of late frost in the air, and the little Rooks shivered in the nest and crept still closer together for warmth.

"When Father Rook came back to sleep, he also got into the nest to escape the cold. All would have been well if they had kept still and quiet, but Mrs. Rook began to ask questions, and Mr. Rook lost his temper, and a fierce quarrel was the result.

"Now, it is a hard thing to quarrel in a very small space without someone getting hurt, and in the fuss which followed the smallest Baby Rook got pushed over the edge of the nest and was hurled to the ground below.

"As soon as the parents found that one of the children was missing they left off quarrelling and spent all the night trying to find the lost baby.

"Alas, when morning dawned, they only found a little dead bird at the foot of the Elm-Tree, and their grief was sad to see.

"But after this the Mother and Father gave up quarrelling altogether and tried to teach their little ones to be kind and good to each other.

"Mrs. Rook looked after the family with greater care, and Mr. Rook spent more time at home, so that when the winds rocked the tall Elm-Tree they all felt safe and happy, and no one ever called them the quarrelsome Rooks again."

CHAPTER XIII

ANOTHER BIRTHDAY

"WELL," said the Elf, "I suppose it's getting time you had another birthday. How old did you say you were?"

"I'm six," replied Miss Wide-awake; "but I've been six so long that I'm sure I must be nearly seven, and I do wish I could have a birthday!"

"So you shall," said the Elf; "only it means that I must go."

"Where to?"

"Back to the Fairy Garden to find a present for you. Have you thought of anything you would like?"

"Oh, am I really to have a present from the Fairy Garden?" cried Miss Wide-awake, clapping her hands. "That will be splendid!"

"Well, it all depends on what you want. Some people like one thing and some another. Most of them go to shops for them, but the nicest presents of all are in the Fairy Garden."

"But I can't go there to choose one, can I?"

"No, I'm afraid you can't—unless——"

"Oh, dear Elf, don't you think I might go there just this once *with you*, if I promised not to touch anything, and only stayed a very little while?"

"But, you know, you *did* touch the Moon-flowers!"

Miss Wide-awake went very red.

"Never mind," said the Elf cheerily; "you weren't as old then as you are now. I'll find out if the Fairies will let you in, to choose your present for a special birthday treat. If not, I shall have to pick one out for you myself. I would like it to be an extra nice one, because after to-day you won't see me any more."

"Not see you any more? Why not?" asked Miss Wide-awake in dismay.

"I'm going away for good. You see, I can't stop after you are seven."

"Then I don't want to be seven, and I don't want a birthday at all!" said Miss Wide-awake, with a sob.

"Hush! hush!" whispered the Elf, "the Fairies will hear you!"

"I don't care if they do!" sobbed Miss Wide-awake, louder than before. "I want you to stay here in the Orchard. I shall never be happy if you go away."

The Elf looked much distressed as the big tears rolled down Miss Wide-awake's cheeks and fell upon the grass.

"Well, well," he said, soothingly, "perhaps it won't be as bad as you think after you've been to the Fairy Garden. We'll go to-night at sunset. The gates are open for a few moments just before the sun sinks behind the Pine-wood. If you stand by the nursery window and watch, you will see the pathway quite clearly; it reaches from the window-ledge right to the garden-gates, and I shall be there, never fear!"

There was some comfort in this, so Miss Wide-awake dried her tears and began to think of the Fairy Garden and all the wonderful things she had heard about it.

When bedtime came, sure enough there was the big red sun setting behind the Pine-wood, just facing the night-nursery window, in a blaze of golden light.

It was a still, warm night, and Nurse left the window wide open, and Miss Wide-awake begged that the curtains might not be drawn so that she could watch the sunset; but, of course, she did not say anything about the visit she was going to pay to the Fairy Garden.

"Bless the child!" said Nurse, as she made ready to leave the room; "what does she want looking at sunsets when she ought to be asleep? It all comes of being an only child and having no one to play with."

But Miss Wide-awake did not hear Nurse's remarks, for she already saw a golden pathway appearing, which reached from the rosy clouds to the nursery window, and it seemed the most natural thing in the world for her to step out into the soft, evening light and walk towards the setting sun.

It was hardly like walking, for she seemed to be floating through the golden air with the Elf at her side.

Then, at last, among the rosy clouds above them, she saw the gates of the Fairy Garden standing wide open, as if quite ready for her to enter, and in another moment she had passed through them.

Never in all her dreams had she pictured

such a wonderful place, or seen such beautiful flowers.

They were not in the least like earth-flowers, but at first she could not tell what the difference was.

But when she looked closer she saw that each blossom was really the face of a little angel-child, sleeping softly as the gentle breezes rocked it to and fro.

Miss Wide-awake dare not speak for fear of waking them, but she watched the Fairies as they flew from flower to flower and kissed each tiny bud so that the petals might unfold.

"Now," said the Elf, "these are all birth-day presents, and you may choose one for yourself."

It was certainly no easy matter to pick one out from all the rest, but with the

Fairies' help she found one which seemed the sweetest bud of all.

"Hurrah!" shouted the Elf. "You'll be quite happy now and not miss me when I have gone."

But Miss Wide-awake did not hear him, for she was clasping the Baby-Blossom in her arms and hurrying back along the golden pathway again.

* * * * *

"Wake up! Wake up!" said a voice in her ear. "It's your birthday to-day, and the Fairies have sent you a Baby Brother!"

Miss Wide-awake tumbled out of bed and stood blinking by a little white cot in her mother's room.

Yes, there could be no mistake, there was the Flower-Baby she had chosen in the Fairy Garden lying cosily asleep, and Miss Wide-awake was allowed to kiss him just once on the tip of his tiny nose. She did not seem at all surprised to see him ; but then, why should she be?

* * * * *

The Elf never comes now to the Orchard, and there are no more stories to be told ; but Miss Wide-awake is as happy as the day is long, for she has her Baby Brother to play with instead !

"Happy as the day is long!" p. 126.

GOOD-BYE TO THE FAIRIES

I

IT'S my birthday! It's my birthday!
I'm seven years old to-day!
I'll soon be quite grown up, so Nurse
And all my Aunties say!

II

But I don't want to be grown up,
Because I once was told
That Fairies are not friends with you
When you are very old.

III

And I'm so fond of Fairies,
  And Elves and tiny things,
And all the little creatures
  That float on fairy wings.

IV

But what d'you think the Fairies
  Told me the other day
They'd give me for a present
  Before they went away?

V

A little Baby Brother—
  All round and soft and pink!
I shall not miss the Fairies
  When I've got him, I think;

VI

So goodbye, Elves and Fairies,
  And all the wee Folk, too,
I know when I am *seventy-seven*
  I'll still believe in you.

THE END.